Sheila

John Gumbs

Published by John Gumbs
Publishing partner: Paragon Publishing, Rothersthorpe
First published 2019
© John Gumbs 2019, London

ISBN 978-1-78222-729-8

Book design, layout and production management by Into Print
www. intoprint. net
+44 (0)1604 832149

Contents

Chapters

Sheila loves her mother very much, but sometimes her mother doesn't know when to stop talking...

1

Listening To Mother

SHEILA STOOD ON the small hill looking at the vast sea. Today, she thought, it is calm, compared to other days when it was quite rough and dangerous. Every time she has a row with her mum she always comes to this little hill to think things out. She will go back home and try to make it up with her mum.

Her mum was a nice lovely woman, but she always likes to argue. And that's one of the reasons why her father left the family. Sheila enjoyed the smell of the sea, and the breeze lightly on her face, then she turned and went back home. She arrived just to meet her mum at the front door.

"Where have you been?" Her mother looked at her angrily. "There's work to be done, get cracking!"

"Alright Mum, I know. I'll get started." Sheila went into the kitchen and started with the washing up.

"You have a nasty habit, Sheila, running away when I'm talking to you," her mother told her.

"Sometimes, Mum, it's unbearable the way you carry on. Give it a break."

"So you too, don't like the way I talk. You're just like your old man. Never want to hear the truth. Always wants to run away." Her mother carried on. "But look at you, *who* brought you up? It was I. Your father abandoned us, and didn't care a damn, don't forget that."

"Yes, I know Mum. But don't get me to try and hate my father, for he too, is a good man. Listen to you now. Give it a rest. Go read a book or something!"

"*Don't* tell me what to do, young woman. Just watch your mouth."

"Anything you say, Mum!"

"Don't be sarcastic!"

Having finished with the washing up, her mum asked, "Are you going out tonight?"

"Yes, I'm going to meet Ricky."

"That boy is a failure. You're going to throw your life away with him?" Her mother waited for an answer.

"He's far better than some of the other boys around here."

Sheila was almost 19, good looking, slim, with dark-brown hair. She had been seeing Ricky for quite a while now, and as far as she knew, it was going okay. Ricky was just a year younger than herself, not as tall as she was, and had ginger hair. Sheila felt safe and good in his company. Her mum, she knew, didn't like him. She had said, "nothing is going to come of that boy." Already she had cast him into prison before she had given him a trial.

"It is I who is dating him, and should know if he's good for me or not."

"The trouble with some of you young girls is that you rush in without knowing what is to come after," her mother said.

Sheila looked intently at her mother and said, "Mum, I know that you were very young when you had me. I know how to take care of myself in that area. Don't worry much about that!"

"That's what they all say," the mother said, "but they all come back with a big belly."

"Watch carefully and see, that won't happen to me. I'm not stupid!"

"Stupid or not, they still come home pregnant. And of course, the mother and father are there, don't you forget that."

"Sometimes I think that some parents become jealous of their children. We ourselves, one day, are going to become parents too. That's the way it all runs!"

So many times before, Sheila had this talk from her mother. She accepted it because all parents were concerned for their children, but Sheila's mother didn't know when to stop. Sheila was dressed up ready to go out, she was still being lectured to. Sheila left her mother and was off with her boyfriend Ricky, to the pictures. She had told her mum what time she would be back.

Sheila found herself pregnant, a few weeks later, but kept it to herself. Her mother, after a while, and the way Sheila was acting, knew that something was wrong. She said to Sheila while they were having breakfast, "By your behaviour, I can tell that there's something wrong with you."

"Nothing to worry about, I'm okay!"

"You're not pregnant, are you?" the mother asked.

"Okay, I'm pregnant. Now you know!"

"Why did you go and let yourself get pregnant now for? Just turning 19, you could have waited."

"From what I've heard, *you* didn't wait, did you?"

"I told you that boy was no good. You just wouldn't listen. Always think that you know best," the mother stated.

"It had nothing to do with Ricky if he was good or bad. It just happened."

"How far are you?"

"A few weeks, I think," Sheila said.

The mother said seriously, "You should have resisted and waited until you were ready for that sort of thing."

"You yourrself know it is not that easy. Some men just can't wait, they want to jump right in as if it's the last day of their lives," Sheila said.

"There's nothing now you can do, he's made his mark," the mother told her.

"That's a rude way of putting it, Mum. For people who are in love it is quite easy for this sort of thing to happen."

"No one gets to my door until I'm ready. I put lock and key on. Your father had to wait. He could not rush me. But I must admit, later, I gave it all over to him," the mother said.

"We're living in modern times, Mum. I've heard of girls going out and coming back the same night pregnant."

"Whatever period we're living in, it's up to the woman. If she says 'no', then the man must accept that. I know some of them do get raped."

Sheila said, "Imagine getting raped by your own

boyfriend. Being forced to do what you don't want to do."

The mother said, "That often happens, and some of them end up still getting married. Would you want to marry someone who raped you?"

"You're saying it as if the boyfriend was an enemy. He is still the boyfriend."

"I just can't follow some of you girls," the mother said.

The next couple of days went without much bother. Sheila met Ricky on the Friday and was planning to tell him that she was pregnant, but changed her mind.

He asked, "How's your mum treating you these days?"

"My mum is still the same, just like all the other good mums, wants to know what's going on."

"You fancy coming to the football match tomorrow?" Ricky asked Sheila.

Sheila was hoping then, that he would have asked her if she'd like to go to a restaurant. She likes football, but a restaurant was more romantic. Ricky, when she first met him, didn't appear to her as a romantic person, so there were some things she never expected from him. A real romantic person would have brought her flowers or a box of chocolates, each time he came to see her. Ricky was in a different class – not the romantic one. His ideas were different, and Sheila knew that very well, but made no fuss about it.

"I'll wait around for you," Sheila told him.

"I'll be spot on time," He told her, kissed her on the lips, and went away.

It was now becoming clear to Sheila what sort of man Ricky was. Thoughts were now coming through her mind to dump him.

On the Saturday afternoon, inside the stadium, watching the local football team play (they were trailing 2-1), Sheila turned to Ricky and said, "It's over!"

Ricky said to her, "No, it's not, there's still a few minutes left."

"Ricky!" she half-shouted, "it's not the game I'm talking about. I mean between you and me."

Ricky said, "You can't be serious. What brought this on?"

"I *am* serious," she told him. "For you and me, it is through."

After the match had ended, Sheila and Ricky parted. It was a terrible moment for Sheila, she was left feeling terrible. It was going to hurt for some time, but she'll get over it. At home, she faced her mother, who, being very observant, saw that something was wrong. She asked Sheila, "Is something wrong, you look a bit sad?"

"I finished it with Ricky!"

"Really?" her mother asked. "Does he know about your pregnancy?"

"I didn't tell him anything."

"Were you afraid to?" the mother asked. "You should have told him and see how he would have reacted."

"He probably would have gotten upset," Sheila said.

"Some men for some unknown reason, don't like to hear such things."

"I have to try and get over him now, and not hurt myself too much," Sheila told her mum.

"You're a young girl, and there are plenty of good romantic men out there."

"Don't forget that I'm pregnant, Mum." Sheila spoke softly.

"Some men don't worry about that," her mum told her. "I'll just wait and see what happens."

""In this world, I can tell you," the mother said, "you have to take your chances."

"Soon, my belly is going to start showing, and men will run away."

"You've got a lot to learn my girl about men," the mother told Sheila. "Meeting the right one is like winning the lottery."

"That will be the day, me meeting the right one, with *this* inside my belly!" Sheila said, rubbing her belly.

"Just wait and see," her mum said.

Sheila went and watched her local football team play. Walking along after the match had finished, this Jaguar car came along, stopped beside her, and the driver said, "Tell me that you're free, and that you're not married!"

Sheila was surprised when she saw the young man. He was a handsome one, just about the same age as her, and was decently dressed. "Are you referring to me?" she asked with a smile on her face.

"You guessed right," he said. "I was looking at you inside the stadium, and took a fancy to you."

"Are you married or have a girlfriend?" Sheila asked him.

"Nothing like that," he said. "Come on, let me give you a lift!"

Sheila took the offer, went and sat next to him in the front. "Did you enjoy the game?" he asked her. "By the way, my name is Anthony, Anthony King."

Sheila said, "I'm Sheila, Sheila Waking."

"Where do you live?" he asked her.

Sheila said, "Not far away, a few minutes drive."

It wasn't long before they came to where Sheila lived. Anthony opened the car door for her, and let her out. "Can I see you again soon?" he asked her.

The words came quickly from her. "Of course, you can!"

"What about next week?" he asked.

"That would be okay," she told him, explaining which day would be best. Anthony drove away.

Sheila opened her front door with a smile on her face, in a happy mood. Her mother was watching TV. Without looking away from the TV, she asked, "Did you enjoy the match?"

"It was enjoyable. The game ended in a draw."

The mother then looked away from the TV, glanced to her left where Sheila was standing, saw the smile on Sheila's face and inquired what it was that made her smile.

"Mum," Sheila started to tell, "this handsome young man drove me home after the football match. He has a Jaguar car."

"Oh! I see," the mum said, "into the big time now, are you?"

"He wants to see me again..."

"Why didn't you ask him in so I could check him out?"

"Give it time, Mum, we've only just met!"

"Has he seen your belly... that you're pregnant... carrying another man's child? I—"

"No, he doesn't know yet. I will break the news to him."

"Bring him home one day, and let me have a look at him," her mother told her. "You know I could tell if a man is good or not."

"Don't go so fast, Mum, I've only just met him."

The next time Sheila met up with Anthony, she invited him back to her home to meet her mum. In the kitchen making the drinks, Sheila's mum said to her, "That one has the touch of being well-bred."

Sheila said, "Mum, there you go, putting the chap way up high. I see him just as a normal bloke."

Back in the living room, the conversation carried on. "So you're from around these areas?" the mum asked. Just as she lifted up the cup to bring it to take some tea, Anthony said, "I'm the youngest son of George King."

Sheila's mum's hand was trembling as she placed the cup back onto the table. "You're having us on!"

George King was a very wealthy man with many department stores, and was owner of all the houses on one particular street.

"I've heard a lot about this George King," Sheila said. "Is he the same one who is your father?"

Anthony said, "Same one!"

The mother said, "This is unbelievable!"

"By God, you're funny as well," Sheila said.

Anthony looked at her and smiled, "I'll take you to a polo match next time."

"You mean that game with horses and sticks?"

"Something like that!"

Sheila was well-liked at the Polo club. She made many friends there, and got many invitations. At the club house, Anthony said to her, "See, you have become very popular. You should have been the one who was playing instead."

"Can't help it," Sheila told him. "In school, it was just the same. I got on well with almost everyone."

"I get the feeling that you're a lucky girl."

"Do you really think so?" Sheila asked.

"Yes," Anthony answered. "I'll stay with you no matter what!"

"You're joking!"

"No, I'm not. I mean what I say," Anthony said straight out.

Sheila said straight away, "You know what! I'm pregnant!"

"But we haven't—"

"I know, it's nothing to do with you. It's from another fellow whom I dumped."

"My! You had me wondering how that was possible when I've only just met you."

"Life is funny eh! Well, I've told you, so now you know."

Anthony said, "That's okay with me. I'll be a good dad to the child."

"Do you really mean that?"

"Not joking at all. I'll be there for you!"

A month passed by after Sheila had been to the Polo Club. She hadn't seen or heard from Anthony. Her mother said to her, "What could have happened to him, you think? Seemed such a nice fellow."

"I don't know!" Sheila answered. "I'll just have to wait and see."

Another two weeks, and there was a letter. Sheila opened it and started reading. Her mother stood by anxious to know what the letter said. After reading for a bit, Sheila said to her mum, "You're not going to believe this! Anthony is in the nick!"

The mother said, "You're joking. What has he done?"

It is to do with his car. It was stolen!"

"Why would he want to steal a car when his father is so rich?" The mother couldn't understand.

"Apparently, he's not in his father's good books."

"So what now?" the mother asked.

"I'll go and visit him, and get the whole story of what's going on," Sheila told her mum. "Maybe it's not his fault, I'll have to find out."

Sheila travelled up to the prison, and visited Anthony. They had a good chat, and she was happy that the whole thing turned out to be a mistake. Anthony promised to drop by when it was all cleared up.

Anthony is out of prison and he came up to see Sheila and her mum. Later, he took Sheila to one of the town's posh restaurants. Sheila enjoyed herself. It was really a romantic evening with Anthony.

She got back home and her mum said, "Well, where did he take you?"

Sheila said, "It was absolutely marvellous, a grand night it was, and the food was first class."

"You've really caught yourself a good one this time. I hope you don't go play the fool and scare him off!"

"I'm not going to scare him off. He knows that I'm pregnant and has accepted it."

"I wonder if he's well in with his family?"

"He must be, even though he says nothing about it.

He's into the Polo club, and has many friends there. And I myself have a few.

"So, my girl, you're heading in the right direction!"

"That's what you wanted, of course! You brought me up well!"

"It is the job of parents to do so," the mother said.

At one of the Polo matches, the friends of Anthony saw Sheila's belly. It was big, and they praised Anthony. He had no intention at this moment to make it known that the child wasn't his. That can wait for the moment, he thought. In the evening there was a barbecue arranged, and Anthony and Sheila sat with friends.

There were royals, high officials, business men well-known in the town. Anthony and Sheila were invited to Pickford Lodge, the home of a great family. It was not a surprise to Sheila that she would get invited to visit such homes, because she always acted in a way that attracted people to her. She knew how to behave and control herself when amongst such high people.

Sheila was also taken to meet Anthony's father, and that went down pretty well. Anthony's father was a man well-known in the town. His dealings with others did him well for he did so honestly. Straight away when he saw Sheila, he took to her. His third wife also took to Sheila.

Anthony knew that there was something special about Sheila. He was glad to have met her, and that she was pregnant with another man's child, didn't bother him at all.

At home her mother said, "Soon you'll be delivering what's inside of you. And then your life will really start."

"It's already started Mum. Life started when I met Anthony. He's really something.

"Do you like Polo matches?" her mother asked her.

"Yes, I do actually. It doesn't bother me, and I love horses."

"Well, that's okay because the likes of Anthony and the others take it seriously."

"It doesn't bother me what sport it is," Sheila said.

"Was the Prince playing at the Polo match?" her mother asked.

"Yes, the Crown Prince was playing."

"Did you chat with him?" the mother asked.

"He was with another group, and I didn't get the chance to meet and talk with him. Why are you so anxious to know?"

"This is a high society game," the mother told Sheila. "You have to understand it, and play it well."

"I think I'm doing fine at the moment," Sheila said.

"Whatever! Your mum is always here,"

"I know, and I'm glad for that!" Sheila told her mum.

"I've got the strong feeling," the mother said, "that you're going to end up one day in the royal household."

"Mum, your feelings could be wrong. What prince is going to waste time on me? I've got Anthony, haven't I?"

"You wait and see girl, you wait and see…"

The time came for Sheila to give birth. She was driven to the nearest hospital, and there she gave birth to a lovely daughter whom she named Evelyn. Many people came to visit her. Then the time came for her to leave and go to her home. At this time, Anthony had gotten a house from his father, and he took Sheila and Evelyn there. Sheila was pleased with the house and its location. Sheila's mother was overjoyed when she came to visit and to see her granddaughter. She felt good within herself now that her daughter had done well for herself.

There were quite a lot of things that Anthony liked about Sheila. She was a very pretty girl, intelligent, and most of all she had this fantastic spirit amongst all people whether high-born or low. He had already made up his mind that he would stay with her and support her child. Children were his first love, so that was no problem to him. But there was one thing he knew, if Sheila would be taken in by one of the princes or higher up ones, he had no chance of getting her back. She didn't seem the type who would be doing such a thing, he thought. Thinking of his dad, who was already on his third wife, Anthony thought to himself, no, that's not for me. I'll stick with the one woman, so long as she will stick with me. Why should I go running round with others? The one is enough – and surely enough.

The Prince was getting increasingly closer to Sheila, and Anthony warned her about it.

2

The Prince's Love

SHEILA FOUND HERSELF pregnant again not long after she had her first child. She went through another nine months, and this time brought forth a boy. They called him Weston. Sheila went to a Polo match without Anthony. She had Evelyn and Weston with her. In the fourth Chukkas, the prince fell from his horse, but didn't hurt himself too badly. There are six Chukkas to play, each Chukkas lasting seven minutes. Sheila enjoyed the match. Anthony heard the news that the prince had taken a fall, but had recovered quickly. In those matches, Anthony had said that such falls are expected.

The prince's birthday party came around, and Anthony and Sheila were invited. They went, and from that evening things were not the same between Anthony and Sheila. Sheila said to Anthony, "I hope you're not jealous because the prince pays lots of attention to me."

"I'm not jealous, but I'm worried you might fall for him," Anthony told her.

"Come on, Anthony. You're a very social person like myself and you know what goes on at all these social do's.

You don't really think that the prince would fall for me, a married woman with two young children?"

"It's quite possible," Anthony said. "Some of them give up their throne just to be with the woman they love."

"This one is not like that. He's intelligent, he's clever, and he knows that the people of the country are behind him, and he won't dare make such a foolish move."

"I've read him carefully, and you, watch out!" Anthony said.

"I thought the prince was your friend!"

"He is," Anthony told her, "but some friends, even the prince, cannot be held back if they want something."

"And you think that the prince wants *me*?"

"Who wouldn't?" Anthony looked carefully at her. "You're a very attractive and beautiful woman with impeccable manners. No one would ever think that you came from a poor family. But you are well-bred, and that's something you have going for you."

"Are you really in love with me, Anthony?" Sheila asked.

"Of course I'm in love with you, who wouldn't be? You have got it all."

"Well, then, don't talk stupidly!" she told him.

"I'm surprised when you were at the football match that no one had noticed you. I was going mad when I saw you," Anthony let her know.

"There were many who were looking at me but weren't brave enough to make a move. That's the trouble with some of you men, you just keep on staring, instead of doing something about it."

*

The prince's birthday party took place in one of the top restaurants. There were many people there. During the feast, the prince made an announcement. He had something important to say. Both Anthony and Sheila were on their toes and shaking. "Now it comes out," Anthony said to Sheila.

"*What* comes out? What're you talking about?"

Later, when the music had stopped playing, and the guests were back in their rightful places, the prince went up to the mike. He said, "I want you all to meet the woman of my life." Then this slender, beautiful woman appeared. Anthony stared, not believing what was happening. He had got it all wrong, thinking that the prince was falling for Sheila. The young girl stood beside the prince, her face lit with a big smile. One could see too that she was well-bred. The guests clapped and cheered. "She's the daughter from the House of Chesford," the prince carried on to say. "Her father is Lord Chesford."

Vivianne was the new love of the prince, everyone knew it. Anthony and Sheila along with the rest of the guests were cheering. They both went over to congratulate him personally. It was all in the papers:

'VIVIANNE CHESFORD, THE LOVE OF THE PRINCE.'

Anthony and Sheila, later, were asked to accompany the prince on his Hebrides trip They accepted. Sheila's mum looked after Evelyn and Weston. While they were away.

The trip around the Hebrides went off well, and everyone enjoyed themselves. Vivianne and Sheila got on well, and visited each other's residences. Anthony apologised for his rude behavior and his foolish remarks about the prince.

Sheila said to him at their home, "Now you have seen that the prince wasn't making any advances towards me. He was just being himself, always social and friendly, and anyway, I was not the only woman he was being so friendly to."

"Yes, I've seen now how stupid I was. Anyway, we all had a nice trip up the Hebrides. The place is really beautiful with all those sandy beaches, and so much wildlife.

Sheila said, "I enjoyed the walking, the sightseeing tour, it was excellent, a great trip."

"There are some people who would never get to see what we saw. Only those who have the money and are capable of travelling will get to see such things," Anthony said. "I was also thinking of ... well ... how about you and I tie the knot permanently?"

There was a smile on Sheila's face. "You're not thinking of—?"

"Yes, I am," Anthony didn't let her finish what she wanted to say. "We should get married!"

"And have more children? You *really* want to get married?"

"It's in my blood. What about you?" Anthony said.

"Shall we do it next year?" Sheila was excited.

"That's settled then!"

The prince had to play in his club, a cricket match, and he invited Anthony and Sheila along. It was a nice fine day, and the prince's team was batting first. They made 150 while the opposing team failed to reach that figure. All in all, it was a great day out with the teas and sandwiches.

The following year Anthony and Sheila got married. In attendance were many people whom Anthony and Sheila knew. The prince and Vivianne attended as well. It was a great wedding. They went over to Germany for their honeymoon. After the honeymoon, Sheila was again pregnant with her third child. Anthony, playing polo, had taken a hit on the shoulder when his horse went down. He was taken to the hospital, and discharged after a few days.

Sheila's third child was exactly a year old. It was a boy and was named Oliver. That same year the prince and Vivianne got married, and the whole country celebrated. The prince later consulted his personal astrologer. The prince was told that Vivianne would not be able to produce an heir. It was not good news for the prince to hear. The love life of the prince and Vivianne was still strong.

At their residence, Vivianne said to the prince, "I was thinking it would be a good thing adopting a child. What do you think?"

The prince said, "It's a good idea, seeing that you can't have any of your own. Are you thinking of going to an adoption service?"

"I was thinking of Oliver," Vivianne said, "he would make a nice family for us."

The prince got a shock when he heard the name. "You don't mean Oliver from Anthony and Sheila? Good Lord, what are you thinking of? They won't part with the child."

Vivianne looked at the prince, smiled and said, "Let me handle it. I'll talk to both of them. I know it's a hard thing, but they'll make a decision."

In the following days, Vivianne spoke with both Anthony and Sheila, and they both agreed to let Oliver be adopted. He would have a much better life, they said, "... and we'll get to see him often."

In the years that flew by, Oliver became a young man, well-loved by all, and was a number one hit with everyone in his country. But with all this, there was one thing against him; he knew he had no chance of becoming king over the country. Even though the people loved him so much, they wouldn't allow it. It didn't worry him. He was happy with the prince and Vivianne, and got to see his real parents often. The prince's mother was even pleased with the way he behaved himself. Oliver was bright, intelligent, gentlemanly always with that pleasing smile attracting people to him. At college he was doing pretty well. For being so young, he was also a lover of horses, and could ride one like an expert. He took part in polo matches, youth horse show jumping, cricket matches and rugby games. It seemed that anything he put his hand to, he was good at it.

Sheila said to Anthony, "I'm so pleased with Oliver, he has turned out to be a good boy. I wonder if he had been the same if he had stayed with us?"

"It is the influence of the prince and Vivianne that turned him to be what he is. I have no regret handing him over to them. All we have to do is bring up Evelyn and Weston the best we can," Anthony told Sheila.

"I agree with you." Sheila told Anthony. "We have done the best thing ever. And we won't regret it."

Two months passed and the prince became king after his father passed away. Later, the coronation would take place; Vivianne would become Queen Consort.

Sheila's mother wasn't pleased when she heard of the adoption of Oliver. She said to Sheila, "They should have gone somewhere else. I'm here and I could take care of him." She later changed her mind, and was very pleased with the way Oliver turned out. He came to visit often. Oliver already knew that he had no chance of getting to the throne. He was happy to be who he was.

On his tour in Germany, the king and Vivianne took Oliver with them As they were coming out of the opera one night, Oliver bumped into this 18-year-old daughter of a well-known German family, and from there on a relationship between them started. They wrote to each other often, and sometimes she would come over to visit.
Both the king and Vivianne were pleased with the relationship.

The king's brother came from overseas, and found that he could not be king.

3

The King's Brother Versus Oliver

THERE SHE WAS, Cecilie, standing next to Oliver on the small balcony where the family of the Royal House paraded themselves. King and queen next to Oliver, with other members at the side of them. Most of the people had come to cheer, but they were more interested in Oliver. The Coronation turned out many people and went down well.

Sheila's mother was very interested in Cecilie; saw her as a real princess – was told that she was – but the house doesn't exist. "You're still a princess for me," she had told Cecilie. Sheila's mum got to know quite a lot about the customs in Germany, and what they ate. She said she'd have to pay a visit herself.

The hunting season started; the king, the queen and Oliver all took part, along with all the other members. They were off to catch the foxes. There were many of them: the Beagle, the Labrador Retriever, the Boykin Spaniel, the Chesapeake Bay Retriever, the German Shorthaired Pointer, the American Foxhound, the Golden Retriever, the Coonhound, the Pit Bull Terrier, the Jack Russell Terrier, the Bloodhound, the Brittany dog, the Wiemaraner, the English Setter and the Irish Setter.

It was learned later, that the king had taken a blow to the head when his horse fell down. He was in a critical state. The queen and Oliver both sat with sad faces when they heard the news. The king's brother was overseas when news came to him. He immediately went back home, and to the hospital, to see his brother. He arrived at the hospital to hear his brother was dead.

The country began mourning for the king, and at the same time they wanted Oliver to be king. The brother of the dead king was next in line, and so he had to take over.

After the funeral had taken place, the country was in a big uproar. Voting had to take place to decide between the king's brother and Oliver. There's no doubt now, Oliver had become a number one hit. He had shown himself to be a very fine gentleman, and there was love for him everywhere. It was hard for any local person to take the throne. There were rules laid down, and this prevented such a thing from happening. With Oliver, it was different. The whole country wanted him to be king. The whole country voted overwhelmingly for Oliver. Being unpopular, the king's brother was defeated. He had quite a number of followers as well, and wasn't going to take it lying down.

Oliver was made king and not by the Parliamentary rules that were laid down. Many of the old officials just couldn't understand it. The people of the country had now chosen their own king. They had no intention of getting rid of the Royal House, they just wanted Oliver to be their king.

The king's brother had many contacts in France. He was now waiting for the coronation of Oliver to take place, and then wait for his chance to cause trouble. Oliver, on the other hand, had to be crowned alone. The princess Cecilie would of course be with him, but she cannot have any title; only members of the Royal House when they get crowned could have a consort.

Oliver had no royal status, but he will become king, and this is partly due to the people of the country. His family would be there but would have no special places allotted to them. They didn't mind at all. Oliver's mum, Sheila and his father Anthony were so proud of him, words failed them. Happy they were, knowing that their son would soon be crowned king of the country.

Vivianne could still stay with the Royal House, but she could not hold the title of Queen Consort anymore. She accepted the new situation, and still would be able to support Oliver.

Oliver's coronation turned out to be one of the most spectacular that the country had ever seen. One had never seen so many troops and policemen, airforce men, and the navy who lined the route from the Royal House to the chapel of crowning. Bands of music were everywhere. The crowds packed like sardines cheered with the flag of the country, waving right to left.

Dead on time, the green and yellow, gold and silver carriage came out. The young, handsome Oliver was in it draped in long thick gold-braided blue robes. The crowd went wild. Oliver waved, and never stop waving until he got to the chapel, and was inside. Helped by his attendants, Oliver went up the few steps, holding his sword that was on his left side safely with his left hand, at the same time controlling the long thick robe with his right. The woollen tunic was then seen, with a cloak over it and fastened to the shoulder with a gold brooch. His train was very long. This was taken care of by two young attendants. Visitors from abroad were already in the chapel along with other high officials, and all the other members of the Royal House. Oliver walked calmly down to the crowning chair and the Archbishop. The main doors were closed.

Among the Royal House members was the King's brother. He had already set his men in place deep below in the crypt; they knew what they had to do.

The crown had already been set on the head of Oliver when six men came up from the crypt, next to the dressing room, into the Coronation hall, and immediately grabbed Oliver and fled. It was very brave what they had done, also dangerous. With so many people in the Coronation hall, they could have been overpowered. But being at the top end, and near to the crypt, it was easy for them.

On the left side of the chapel, there was a double wall adjoining another great old building. The front part of the chapel was crowded with people and troops. The men had already left the building with Oliver without being apprehended. Troops at the front area couldn't do anything. The front doors were opened, and the attendants shouted, *"King Oliver has been kidnapped."*

There was a lot of muttering amongst the crowd. Normally, when the front doors were opened, the crowd expected to see the crowned king. The news went through the crowd right up to the Royal House.

Having taken King Oliver away, the men had stripped him of his robes, took him to the back by the double wall and into a police car that had been waiting there. But they were surrounded immediately by other police cars, and King Oliver was taken back to the chapel.

Out he came at the front door fully dressed as King. People were merry, they were glad, they had their King Oliver back. The carriages rode up to the Royal House. King Oliver was again waving to the left and to the right as the carriages moved along.

Inside the Royal House, he was told how lucky he was to be rescued. Everyone was pleased that he was safe, and was now King.

Up to this time no one suspected that the king's brother had anything to do with the kidnapping of King Oliver. The way it took place was rather clumsy, not professional at all. Anyway, the rest of the procession still went off well.

Not long after the coronation, King Oliver, along with Cecilie, visited Canada. While there, both of them decided it was time to get married. King Oliver was also a big hit with the people in Canada.

The country now had three massive bills on its books: the funeral of the old king; the coronation of Oliver; and soon, the wedding of King Oliver. Again, the country was celebrating and enjoying themselves when the wedding of King Oliver and Cecilie took place.

After the wedding, they both took a Caribbean tour. The islands they visited on the tour were pleased to see their new king. They learned that he was not of the Royal House, but born of local parents. The children in the schools waved their flags as the King drove by.

Back at home the king was out in the wilds hunting. Lying low in the bushes with his gun pointing up in the sky, waiting for birds to fly by, the king's brother, being on the hunt as well, was not very far. He pointed his gun towards King Oliver, and one of the attendants, seeing this, jumped him. The gun fell to the ground. No one else but the attendant knew what the king's brother intention was. Everything became clear when they got back to the Royal House. From that day onward, he was being watched carefully.

King Oliver along with Vivianne were in the library of the Royal House when the king's brother came in. He wasn't in a good mood. Vivianne saw that, and excused herself. The king's brother sat down in a chair next to King Oliver. Outside there were two attendants.

"What do you want to talk about?" the king asked.

"Family business!"

"Oh! And that is?" The king closed the magazine he had been looking through. The king's brother said, "You're not from the Royal House. You're from an ordinary family."

"Ordinary family? What does that mean? I am now King of the country, am I not?"

"This is because the people are deceived. They have abandoned the solid building for a shaky one."

The King said, "We are living in a society where the majority rules. To me that is fair and just. And if you had read your history correctly, you would see that the people of the country were the ones who had the power. Only in certain cases could the king or queen do whatever they like."

The king's brother got up out of the chair, moved across to the portrait of King George III, looked at it, then turned around and said, "I am from the line of the Royal House. You have stolen my inheritance."

"I have stolen nothing, my dear fellow. I am a citizen of the country and they have found me suitable enough to be king more than they have found you."

The king's brother said, "King George III built up a great library. What are you going to build up? Or may I say *tear down?*"

"As you know yourself, I'm busy with clubs for the youth. Our young people need good recreational clubs to inspire them."

Two servants came in and asked if there was anything needed. There was nothing needed, so they left. The king's brother continued, "Just look at all these portraits in this library, they are all my ancestors."

"You know well that I'm not from any Royal House, I'm a local person, but I do have albums with my family pictures," King Oliver said.

"*Albums!* Look just beyond you, nothing but albums there. You'll spend weeks upon weeks looking through them."

"What are you getting at?"

"I'm trying to show you that there's a big difference

between my house and your house," the king's brother explained.

"Why can't you and I head for peace?" the king told the king's brother. "That would be good for the country, and they might turn towards you again."

"Are you serious?" the king's brother asked. "Once the country has made its decision, that's it, they don't turn back." He went over to the portrait of King John, Richard I's brother. "The country didn't like King John, but he still became king, and didn't rule properly. He was very good though in recording events and things. Militarywise, he was hopeless. He lost a few battles. You're lucky, you haven't got so much power as these kings had in the olden days."

"He wasn't that bad, I mean King John. Things just didn't go well for him. That's the way life runs sometimes."

"Your father is a very good horseman, and you have turned out even better than him. I tell you what I'll do, I challenge you to a horse cross-country competition. If you win, we shall forget the hard feelings and become friends, agreed?"

"You mean going over all those obstacles? That is cross-country jumping... I... I will take you on!" the king replied.

"Okay, I'll get it sorted out," the king's brother said.

Outside in the garden just before lunch Vivianne was there, so was King Oliver and the king's brother, sitting at the table. Vivianne said, "I am so pleased that the two of you are becoming friends."

The king's brother said, "Ah! We have a contest to go through first, cross-country jumping."

"Are you *mad*?" Vivianne was surprised to hear of the contest. "One of you, maybe both, are bound to come back with broken bones."

King Oliver said, "It's a good challenge, it will bring out the best of both of us. The horsemanship, the endurance, and the skill."

The king's brother said, "We have to get cracking, and put in some practice. The course is not that long, only 4000 metres."

King Oliver asked, "Has anyone in the Royal House had such a contest before?"

"Not really! But they've done European and World Championships."

"Great to hear that," King Oliver said. "We're no champions, and God only knows what will happen on the day."

The king's brother said, "Being such a good horseman, the course should be easy."

"You're forgetting that there are obstacles to cross over. It's totally different on the flat," King Oliver said.

"Yes, I see what you mean."

*

King Oliver and the king's brother spent weeks upon weeks practising; then the final day came for the contest. Most of the Royal House were there to watch, along with many horsemen from top clubs. There was a small group of people who at the time were visiting the country. They had come over from the Dutch Royal House. There was a beautiful princess among them, princess Ilka.

Everyone was asking, "What is it with this Oliver? Why is he so popular? No one knew the answer. He was just who he was. He had everything. The Dutch were amazed about the contest, even some officials as well. If King Oliver were to win, he and the king's brother would become friends; but if King Oliver were to lose, there'd be no friendship between them – a rather strange contest.

The course was well set out. It wasn't hard for the spectators to see the horses at the different obstacles. All the judges were there and ready. King Oliver and the king's brother were on their thoroughbreds, in the required kit and ready to start. King Oliver won the toss and went first. It is good if they can do the course without any penalties. The one with the lowest score is the winner.

King Oliver made it over a couple of fences. He came to a boulder with a water ditch. The horse went over the boulder well, but as it landed in the water, it flung King Oliver over its head and into the water, still holding the reins. He got back on the horse immediately, and was on his way again. King Oliver had to jump across a ditch which he did without any bother. He completed the course and saw his points.

The king's brother was next to ride. The king's brother got over the water ditch easily, and went on to the next obstacle. Tackling one of the logs, the horse refused to jump. This cost him some time as he had to go around it. He was slowed down going through the small stream. He lost quite some time there. The hills and fences he did well. Finishing the course, he saw his points. He was disgusted with himself, but went straight over and shook hands with King Oliver.

From that moment on they were like buddies. It happened that when the king's brother came to the king, there were also the Dutch princess and some members of the family talking with the king. King Oliver introduced the king's brother to the princess.

"So you are Prince James!" Princess Ilka said. "I've heard and read a lot about you." The princess spoke good English.

"Yes, I'm Prince James, and it is nice to meet and speak with you."

"Thank you!" the princess told him. "By the way, you did a very good course in the cross-country. It was unlucky for you though to have lost the contest."

"Yes, it was rather unlucky!"

King Oliver's family were there too. They had watched the contest with Vivianne, and were greatly pleased when the King won. Now they are staying to watch the real competition.

The horse cross-country jumping now finished, that same evening there was a get-together in the Royal House. Prince James along with King Oliver, Vivianne, Princess Ilka, and some other members spoke about the event.

"If I had won," Prince James begun, "I would not be here talking to the king, we would still be at each other's throats."

"No, no, not me," the King said, "I would not be trying to do you harm. But anyway, I'm glad we can now see clearly, and forget the past."

"Vivianne said to the king, "Your riding was brilliant apart from that fall in the water ditch."

"I had him line up properly," the King told them, "but for some unknown reason, it went wrong."

"But you still thrashed me," Prince James said.

"That was pure luck on my part," the King said, and laughed.

Vivianne said, "I'm glad you both came out of it without

any problems, I mean like broken bones and such like."

Prince James turned to Princess Ilka and asked, "How's the beautiful flowers over in the Netherlands?"

The princess looked at him and smiled. "They're growing up pretty well. They are a sight to see!"

"The tulips aren't they?"

The princess said, "Yes, they are. Can be seen in quite a number of places. Should you come over for a visit, you'll get to see them all."

"I've never been to your country, but my father has. I hear that the people there are very friendly."

It had been arranged that after the wedding and the Caribbean tour, Cecilie would return to her homeland for four weeks, then return. Oliver had kept her informed of all that had happened, and he was waiting for her arrival soon.

"Yes, they're hospitable, helping each other as best as they can. I say, King Oliver, when is your lovely wife due back? I miss chatting with her."

"Not very long now," King Oliver replied.

"You both are welcome to come and visit when she gets back; and you Prince James are also invited," Princess Ilka told them.

Both King Oliver and Prince James thanked the princess, accepting her invitation. Vivianne was also invited.

Cecilie came back from Germany, and King Oliver let her into all that had happened. Princess Ilka and her party had already departed for their home. Cecilie was pleased to hear that King Oliver had won the contest and there was peace between the two men.

Love in the air for Prince James and Princess Ilka.

4

Prince James And Princess Ilka

THE TRIP OVER to the Netherlands was a bit turbulent, but they arrived safely, and were escorted back to the Dutch Royal House. King Oliver and Cecilie, Vivianne and Prince James were shown quite a lot in their short visit there. They saw many of the tulip fields, shown the different canals of the Amsterdam waterways. They visited the palace Northeinde, Madurodam, Peace Place, the Gemeentemuseum, and many other interesting places.

Back on their home ground, the King and the rest of the Royal House could not stop talking about their trip to the Netherlands. It was fabulous. It had also become clear to some members of the Royal House that there was something brewing up between Prince James and Princess Ilka. They seemed to have a liking for each other. That would be great having the Dutch Royal House and the Royal House of Prince James combining. Prince James wasted no time and as soon as he got back home, he got in touch with her. They were on the line for a very long time.

*

Princess Ilka was very good herself on a horse, and loved them very much. Prince James was surprised when he heard of it. He was thinking now, they both could ride out to the countryside and have a picnic, but first, he must invite her over.

It wasn't long before Princess Ilka came over from the Dutch Royal House, and both she and Prince James along with some attendants went out to the countryside for a picnic.

Riding their horses side by side, they trotted along the small lane dividing the fields with stones lining both sides. It was a beautiful day, and they came upon a field with not many trees. The scene was whitish-yellowish-greenish, real spectacular. In the distance were a few trees, while close by was this lone one. It was tall, and its branches spread out like an umbrella. It was then decided that the picnic would be held under this tree. The sky had a colour of deep blue with patches of white clouds here and there. Birds flew into the tree while others were in the field hopping around, and then flying away. Prince James and the princess came under the tree, gave their horses to the attendants, and went to the picnic area. Prince James and Princess Ilka sat down and tucked in. Princess Ilka said, "Your countryside is very beautiful. It is like a painting when you look at it."

"I saw some beautiful scenery in your country as well. Only that over here there are many hills and valleys, while your country is flat."

"That is true," Princess Ilka said, "we haven't got such big hills as you have here in Britain."

Prince James looked at Princess Ilka, "What a marvellous charming name you have!"

"It was my mother who picked it out."

"She's done well," the prince said. "I don't think that there are many people with that name. I notice also that you have a very strong love for horses, and you ride them pretty well."

"I grew up loving horses. They are excellent animals. You yourself are not a bad rider, and you must love horses as well."

"Back in your home place, I saw a beautiful painting of you when you were much younger. It is a brilliant painting," Prince James said.

"Yes, I know the one you mean. It was done when I was 13 by one of our famous artists."

"Even now your beauty hasn't faded," Prince James said, looking at her more deeply.

"But your countryside is still more beautiful," she told him.

"I don't think you can compare the two. I would always pick you."

"That's a great compliment, thank you."

"I suppose that you're a great lover of music as well."

"I am. I play the piano. I will let you hear me play when we get back."

"Mozart, Beethoven or Vivaldi?" the prince said.

"Beethoven yes, and sometimes Elgar."

"I have to listen because I cannot play a note," the prince told her.

"Before I go back home, I shall teach you how to play," Princess Ilka told the prince.

The prince replied, "I warn you now, you're going to have much trouble teaching me!" Then he laughed.

The princess laughed too, and said, "We shall see."

There were three trees in the distance, about five minutes walk. The prince told his attendants that they were finished with the picnic, and would be going for a walk to stretch the legs. Off they went, the prince and the princess down to the trees. Another small road on their right led up to where the trees were. Just beyond the trees was a small hill.

Reaching the trees, the princess took a good look around and said, "Yes, it is really beautiful!"

Prince James said, "You wait until you see up in Scotland!"

"Are you planning to take me there, James?"

"It will be a pleasure to take you there and let you see all the hills and valleys." They looked around some more, got their horses from the attendants and were ready to make the trip back.

Along the way back, the princess said to Prince James, "That was an excellent picnic, with a most romantic view. Do you often do that?"

"Only for a special person," the prince told her.

Two days later, Prince James and Princess Ilka, accompanied King Oliver, Cecilie and Vivianne to open a youth club. Prince James and Princess Ilka saw more and more of each other until they finally fell in love and got engaged. The marriage would take place in the Netherlands. It was set for a year later.

Sheila's mum opened the brown envelope, and it almost fell from her hands when she read what it said: King Oliver was coming to make a personal visit. *"Sheila!"* she half shouted, "you won't believe it, but your son is coming to visit us."

"Really!" Sheila asked. "How do you know?"

"It's here in this official letter, with the king's seal on it."

"That son of mine," Sheila said. "Just marvellous! Does it say when?"

"In three weeks time, the date is here."

Permission had been given for Prince James to get married. The marriage would take place in the Netherlands, and Prince James would be living there after becoming a Dutch National.

Meeting up with Princess Ilka again, she told him everything about her Royal House, and all the rules laid down to get married. They were all in the Library in the Royal House of England. "It is better you than me learning that language," King Oliver told Prince James.

Vivianne said to Cecilie, "Let's hear a word from you in your own language."

"This word I'm going to say is 'I' in the English language, and you say 'Ik'. Say that James!" Princess Ilka turned to Prince James.

Like a kid in school, Prince James repeated after the princess and said, "Ik."

"See," she said, "it's not that hard to learn. Now say, 'Ik houd van jou."

Prince James said, "Ik houd van jou."

"Do you know what it means?" she asked him.

He answered, "Something to do with love!"

"Yes," she said. "Very clever. How did you know that?"

"Just a guess!"

"Well, it was a good one. It actually means, *I love you.*"

Princess Cecilie from the Old Royal House of Germany said, "In German, we say, 'Ich liebe dich.' Oliver already knows a few sentences."

In the street where King Oliver's parents live, people were already hanging up banners, and putting chairs and tables out for the following day, when the King would be visiting his parents.

A line of cars came the following day escorting the king. There were many people waving and shouting, "God save the King," as he entered the house where his parents lived. After some time, he came out, sat at a table with some young people, then he walked quite a number of tables and talking to others. The line of cars left the street with the people still enjoying themselves. The papers were full of the event the next day.

Even though Prince James didn't become king, he was still part of the Royal House, and under the power of the people of the country. He knew that they had a say in whom he married and what he did. They liked it very much that he fell in love with a Dutch princess. The people were behind him for his wanting to marry the Dutch princess. There is also another thing, Prince James would have to learn the Dutch language and become a Dutch National in order to be of the Dutch Royal House.

*

A year had passed and the time came about for the marriage between Prince James and Princess Ilka to take place. People in both countries were glued to their TVs.

The civil ceremony started at 10:45 am. Princess Ilka wore a gorgeous white silk dress with a long train, beautifully embroidered. She had three bridesmaids. Princess James wore his army dress being once a part of the Royal Infantry Battalion. He had the normal sash across his chest. They both looked their best on this day.

They also had to attend the Church ceremony, and that went down as planned. As soon as the doors were opened, and all the guests and officials already seated, Prince James on the left side of the princess, walked her slowly down to where the ceremony would take place. After this ceremony had ended, the coach took them on tour through the different places, and then to the palace where the Royal balcony was.

King Oliver, Cecilie and Vivianne were all pleased with how it went off. The wedding over, King Oliver and the rest flew back to their own Royal House. There were great celebrations going on all over the Netherlands, and in King Oliver's country. Soon, Prince James and Princess Ilka would be leaving for their honeymoon up in the Scottish Highlands.

King Oliver was very young when he saw on TV the 'King's Parade'. He watched it with enthusiasm. His parents explained quite a lot about it to him. There are reports that the 'King's Parade' started way back when King Charles II was in power. In 1748 it became officially known as the parade marking the king or queen's birthday. It then became an annual event after George III became king. It was also organised for troops to recognise their regiments and flag colours when they were going into battle.

Just before the ceremony started, Evelyn, King Oliver's sister had met up with this young gentleman from the countryside. He was new to city life. Evelyn told him that she was the king's sister. He didn't believe her at first, but while in the capital, he found out that it was so. The young gentleman's name was Cristian. He came from a good family who owned lots of land.

King Oliver hadn't dreamt that he would this day be king and inspecting the troops. He had seen it all year after year; an extraordinary traditional ceremony. In the carriage with Cecilie and Vivianne, they rode down to where the parade would take place. The other carriages followed with members of the Royal House. The streets were lined with policemen and soldiers and navy and army personnel; and packed with civilian onlookers.

With all the regiments lined up on the parade ground, it was a spectacular sight. The music started as soon as the King's coach entered the area. They struck up, *"God save the King."* The dais where the king would sit and watch the parade was there, with the spectators standing behind it. Evelyn, Cristian and her family were there waiting to watch the parade. All the carriages were now in, and the high officers started the parade. One of them came up to the king and saluted, then the whole parade presented arms. King Oliver stepped down from the dais, and was ready to inspect the first regiment. Many soldiers in the first Regiment to the dais started trembling for when the King's coach came to the parade ground, it went straight to the dais.

With other king's parades gone by, the king or queen stayed in the coach as it went along the troops. These soldiers in the first Regiment knew that there was something strange about that. They were right. King Oliver had spent three years in the army as a local boy. He enjoyed it and loved the discipline. Now that he was king, he had done well so far, and was well-loved by the people. He intended now to inspect the Regiment soldier by soldier. No sooner had the king come to the first soldier in the front row, starting from the left, the fifth soldier down in the line, buckled forward, and became a heap on the ground. The soldiers were now with their arms in their right shoulders, ready for inspection. The king asked the first soldier his name, and the soldier replied immediately his name. The king spotted some white stuff on the left side of the soldier's bearskin cap, and the soldier's name was written down by one of the officers following.

Before the king had finished inspecting the front line, three soldiers had fainted down in the ranks. Funny, they weren't taken away, but were helped up, and back in their positions. Ten soldiers were put on charges because of being scruffy. After inspection, King Oliver went back to the dais, and watched the rest of the parade.

Evelyn and Cristian and Weston enjoyed watching it. Next year, another regiment would be picked to be inspected, so they will know what to look out for. The five regiments along with the musicians put on a grand show, and the King told them in a speech that it was a fantastic performance.

5

Weston And The Olympics

WESTON WAS NOW a sportsman, and was doing well. He was down at his club training when two girls came in and sat in the stands, He had seen them come in and became interested. After working out with a few runs around the track, he went over and approached the girls.

"Hi," he said. "I'm Weston. I see you're interested in sports."

"We are! Especially athletics." They told him their names, Laura and Doris. They liked watching football too.

"What are you training for?" Doris asked.

"The 400 metres," Weston said, "and I have to train very hard."

"We can see that," they both said. "It is a tough race."

Weston said, "I need to have speed with this race. So, in training, I do lots of sprints. I run about 300 metres as hard as I can, then I rest for about 15 minutes; then I start it all over again. After that, I turn to short runs like 150 metres and hurdles. All this I do for strength. Then for real fitness, a few hundred metres. I have to do all this three times a week."

Laura said, "It's a really hard workout, but if you want to be the Olympic champion, you have to stick it no matter what."

"That's exactly what I'm doing. What do you girls do in your evenings?" Weston asked them.

Doris answered, "Friday nights we are in 'Bright Nights Disco' on the High Street, half an hour from here. Do you like discoing? It's fun, keeps you fit as well."

"I hope you girls haven't got boyfriends!"

Laura said, "No, we are free. No boyfriends at all."

Doris said, "We'll see you later then."

They said goodbye to Weston and left. Weston went back over to his trainer. He asked him, "Who were they?"

"Just a couple of friends," Weston said.

The trainer said, "I want you to be concentrating on your training for it is very important. You're getting into top form now, and that Olympic title will be yours."

Weston found himself on the High Street outside Bright Nights Disco. He had no real plans of going inside. He could not make up his mind if he should go in or not. But he remembered he had promised them that he would come. The words of his trainer were still in his ears, and he knew they made sense. If one wants to be the Olympic champion, one has to discipline oneself, and be careful how one treads.

The big man outside the door moved away as Weston found himself in a big lighted area with music blaring. Over in front of him, he spotted Laura and Doris at the bar, seated on high stools. When they saw him they greeted him and asked him to get a stool, which he did. Weston talked and danced with the girls up until midnight, then he left for home.

The following week in training, Weston did a good time of 44.30 – that was pretty good. Still, the training went on. A big competition took place in Brussels and Weston came first in the 400 metres, clocking up a time of 44.40. Both the trainer and himself were very pleased. At another meeting in Germany, he did well. While he was training again, Laura came on her own to watch. Doris had to work. After training, Laura and himself walked back up to a cafe, went inside and started chatting. Laura was taking a fancy to Weston. He sensed it, but didn't mind. She said to him, "You're doing pretty well with your times. That is really fantastic!"

"I'm getting close to where I want to be. I hope to hit my target on time." He asked about Doris, and she told him that she was at work, couldn't get away. Laura was just a bit taller than Doris, and very pretty in the face. She was very communicative, easy going, and full of laughs. Doris was the more serious type.

Laura said to Weston, "There's a football match on Saturday. Want to come?"

"Fine with me," Weston said. I have no training on that day. I'll pick you up half an hour before."

"Okay then, see you!"

Going out a few times with Laura, Weston became her steady boyfriend. They went out many times to the disco, to the football and athletic meets. They travelled short distances visiting relatives.

One Sunday, after watching a football match with the club playing at home, Weston and Laura went to the general park where there were many people. It was a beautiful sunny day, not too hot but just right for lazing about. Beneath a small tree, they both rested. Weston said, "That was a terrible match the club played today!"

"Yes, they got beat. They weren't playing their best," Laura answered. "Are you any closer to the time you want to get to?"

"I've come down to 43.10," Weston said. "My trainer was over the moon, he couldn't believe it."

"I am also delighted that you've achieved that time." Laura reached over and gave him a kiss. Weston took hold of her and kissed her passionately. She said, when he had stopped, "Wow! That's a 400 metre kiss. That's an Olympic medal!" He was ready to give another one, but didn't. She was waiting for it as well. Weston said, "If I win the Olympics, I will give you a real treat."

Laura smiled, she said, "Weston, you'll get from me the treat of your life. I know that you have it in you, and can deliver. Do it for me."

With more disciplined training, Weston kept the time down to 43.10. That was good enough to see him through the finals. He knew he had to go through the heats, and was preparing himself for that. A couple more months and the Olympics came around.

*

The stadium was packed as usual. Weston felt in good shape, he was super-fit, ready to show the spectators what he was made of. Last minute warnings were given to him by his team. He must make sure of not getting into any false start. Concentration was very important. Get into his mind that he has already run the race, by tracing the whole track. Weston was ready.

King Oliver opened the Olympics with a grand speech. Weston sailed through the heats, through the semi-finals, and ended up as one of the eight finalists. Everyone waited until the time came for the 400 metres. It was always a spectacular race to watch. The eight contestants were already in their lanes. Weston had lane six. Everyone was nervous. The stadium watched and waited patiently.

A voice came over the small speakers that were in the lanes, saying, "On your marks," then a pause, "set," and then the starting gun went off. The competitor in lane one moved before the starting gun went off, and was immediately disqualified. Nerves were now high among the athletes. The stadium was still as the athletes got down for the second time. The starting gun went off and they were away. Weston had a steady pace, then went into a beautiful rhythm. Around the 150m mark, he had another athlete right beside him.

Weston's grandmother, sitting next to her daughter Sheila, with her grandchildren close by was shouting her head off, yelling, shaking her head, calling out Weston's name repeatedly. *"COME ON WESTON! COME ON! IT'S YOURS, WESTON KEEP GOING!"*

At the 200 metres mark, Weston kicked, and went into a stride that would shake his opponent off. All in the stadium were so pleased with watching this 400 metres race. The last 100 metres Weston was in a strong position heading for the tape. He came in with a beautiful bow with his head in a time of 43.13. He didn't beat the World record or match it, but he was the Olympic champion.

Sheila was down at the track and hugging and congratulating her son. Laura was there too, and when it was her turn, all the people watched, and thought she'd never stop kissing him. As he moved along, people congratulated him. Weston was the Olympic champion of the 400 metres race.

*

Up in the Scottish Highlands Prince James and Princess Ilka were enjoying their honeymoon. With their attendants and nearing Inverness, Princess Ilka said to Prince James, "You were absolutely right. The beauty of Scotland is overwhelming. Even on wet days. It is beyond words."

"I'm glad you are enjoying it. Soon, we'll be coming to the lake where the Loch Ness monster is supposed to live."

"Loch Ness monster?" the Princess asked. "I've never heard of it."

"Probably because you're too young. But there's a story that goes way back. This monster is supposed to be from prehistoric times."

"Do you believe that James?"

"Many people reported that they have seen it," the prince told her. "It's supposed to be long and has a head."

"Let's hope we see it today," she said. "I have my camera ready."

They were on the lake for some time and hadn't seen anything strange to do with 'Nessie' as the Loch Ness monster was called. Princess Ilka was an enthusiastic young woman. She didn't mind stretching her feet a few kilometres to see the beauty of the area. They spent some time in the Inverness castle grounds, looking around.

One of the mountainsides was very steep. Prince James and Princess Ilka decided to walk up it. The view was breath-taking. They could have walked around the track, but this day, they felt adventurous. There were many trees on this side of the mountain. With a couple of attendants in front, and others behind, they started out.

Half-way up, Princess Ilka putting her right foot forward, slipped, fell, and started sliding downwards. She was very lucky because there were many trees around. As she rolled down, she slammed into a tree, and it was her rucksack that took the blow. Her foot was a bit hurt, but nothing to worry about. It was carefully examined by the medic, and found to be okay; no break or anything like that. Her back too, was in good condition. Resting for half an hour, she started out again, and this time made it to the top without any more incident.

The following day they visited the Cathedral, the Botanic gardens. Other days they visited a few castles. They took also the route from Nairn to Cawdor which is about 8 kilometres. They saw some interesting things along the way, and of course the castle at Cawdor.

6

Countryside Wedding

IT WAS SHEILA's birthday, the family was there. Evelyn with Cristian; Weston with Laura; Anthony, Sheila's husband was there, and her mother. King Oliver was in Germany. He spoke to his mother over the phone. The table they were seated at was long and had 12 chairs around it. Having looked at all the cards and presents she had received, Sheila's mum brought the food in. Others began to help.

Half-way through the meal, Evelyn announced that she and Cristian were ready to get married, and that she would be living out in the countryside. She will not visit the towns and cities like she used to do. She said she'd probably visit once in a while. Anthony's father came later with his wife. They all chatted right down until it was late.

The morning sun pitched its light across the fields making them look yellowish. With a bunch of trees here and there leading up to the small hillside, it was an amazing sight. From a distance you could see the four three-storey buildings, and the outer barns. One of those buildings would house Evelyn and Cristian after they've been married.

There were very many acres owned by Cristian's parents. Evelyn had already seen the countryside a few times and loved it. There was no doubt in her mind at all about settling there. The outdoor life appealed to her. She could see herself running after and feeding the chickens, feeding the pigs and the horses. All this she didn't mind doing.

Cristian was a nice man, very lovable, hard-working, and loved his family very much. Evelyn knew she had picked the right man. She got on well too with his family, and she never felt out of place. They treated her well.

The area around the houses was arranged and set up well for the wedding. There were many who attended from the outlying farms. Her own family was there too. King Oliver, Cecilie and Vivianne also attended. Her mother, her grandmother, Weston and Laura; her father and some of his family came. Her grandfather on her mother's side wasn't there. She knew the story since she was young, and realised that such things took place.

On the day, it was a grand countryside wedding. Evelyn wore a gown down to her shoes which were white; sleeves long and wide; it had a circular shape in the front with an embroidered pattern. Cristian wore a smart grey suit. The ceremony went down well, with the music being played with guitars. The day was beautiful and everyone had a good time. Inside the big round white tent where the reception was held, it was spectacular to look on how the chairs and tables were laid out. There was no big wedding cake as normal weddings have, but the cakes and other foods were fine. Before the reception was over, and they had their dances, and greeted everyone, they were whipped away to the Cotswolds to begin their honeymoon. They would stay in a luxurious farm house, with various amenities. Chipping Norton, the market town, wasn't far away.

Evelyn and Cristian were now enjoying their honeymoon. What beautiful scenery. The white painted stones lining the villages; and the hills with their green foliage captured them. Some places around were really a dream. The houses covered with climbing plants; and the windows with their many frames, caught the eye quickly.

In their luxurious farmhouse, Cristian asked Evelyn how she felt now it was all behind her. She smiled, came close to him, kissed him, and said, "I really enjoyed it, I did. It was fantastic!"

"You have no regrets?" he asked.

"No, none. I am happy. I don't think that there's any woman in the world happier than I am."

It is the end of the honeymoon and Evelyn and Cristian were back and around the family once more. It was the custom among the farmers to visit each other's farms, and exchange and buy whatever each one needed. There was also the market town of Chipping Norton.

Evelyn was now very busy with her own farm helping the family in every way she could. She had meetings with the other women around the area, and they would plan trips to the different market towns. Cristian saw how busy his wife was, and she was loved by the other women. He was pleased about that and told her so.

*

A year on and great news came about. Evelyn was pregnant with twins. Everyone in the family was pleased to hear the news. Even King Oliver sent a letter of congratulations to her. The following year Evelyn bore twins for Cristian and gave them the names of Henry and Sophia. Her mother and grandmother were over the moon.

7

Prince Bert. King Oliver's Visit To Germany

PRINCE BERT WAS the son of the old King's sister Alice. He was a rough, tough one. He had no real respect for the Royal House. Falling in love with married women who have two or three children, and estranged from their husbands. Prince Bert had been in the Army, and was a big hit among his comrades. King Oliver had been watching him and his behaviour, and decided to have a chat with him. Prince Bert had left the married woman with her children and had hooked himself up with a divorced actress.

Inside the library, King Oliver said to him, "Your conduct is very upsetting. Can you not try to see how important it is for the Royal house that you act in a good way."

"Are you saying that I cannot fall in love with whom I want to?"

King Oliver shifted in his chair, looked at Prince Bert more seriously and said, "We fall in love with whomsoever we want to fall in love with. But you are from the Royal house, and that means that we are always in the public eye.

Don't you know that the whole world reads about us?"

"Yes, I know that! This woman is special to me, whether she's divorced, an actress or whatever."

"You'll have to give her up, Bert, and look for someone more suited for this house."

"You're not serious, are you? Asking me to give up the woman I love!"

"That is *exactly* what you'll have to do if you want to remain with the house." King Oliver said.

"I will leave this forsaken house, and go with my love."

"The choice is yours, Bert, but think it through carefully before you do something that you'll later regret."

"I won't regret it. I'll go and live a normal life with the woman I love. In this house, the photographers are like flies around you. Your every move is recorded. That's not for me anymore. I am leaving."

"You sure that that is what you want?" King Oliver asked him.

"Yes, I'm sure. Soon, you won't be seeing me around here anymore. Definitely, I am going to leave."

"Kings and queens and their families have kept this Royal house going; and this was achieved through integrity, through good manners, and good behaviour. True, there were some who could not keep the standard. You have turned out to be one of those who are not able to face the public, uprightly and boldly. To be in the Royal house or to be a member of it takes quite a lot. Not just anybody can withstand the pressure," the king told him.

Prince Bert left the Royal house, went and lived with the divorced actress. Cecilie heard of what had happened and said to the king, "Oh! What a terrible thing! Why could he not see sense, and stayed?"

"He wants to live his life that way, and there's nothing more that we can do."

Vivianne was a bit upset from what had taken place. No one ever thought that Prince Bert would have acted that way.

King Oliver was now getting ready to depart to Germany. Cecilie and Vivianne would accompany him along with his usual staff. He would stay at the big camp where he would meet the Minister President of Germany, and watch a passover of military aircraft. On his list was a small unit close to the Dutch border. Everyone was already getting prepared months before. The guard of honour was being taken care of in both regiments. They remembered the King's parade and what took place there. So they were well-informed, and ready to put on a good show.

At one of the bases, the king will be given a tour of the beautiful Vulcan plane. The small regimental unit was now setting the whole camp to make it look presentable for when the king should arrive. Men and women were busy in their offices. Outside the white stones lining both sides of the road were re-painted. A helicopter took the king and his staff from the Royal house to the airfield where he would depart from.

It was a nice lovely day when King Oliver landed at the airfield in Germany. Many cars were to transport him and his staff away. First, he inspected the guard of honour that was laid on for him; all went well. The following day he watched a football match between men and women. Then he watched soldiers climbing ropes and going over barriers, and through muddy waters. Another day, he was taken to look at the Vulcan on the airbase. He stood underneath it, and still there was space above his head. Seated in the co-pilot's seat, he looked at all the switches and instruments. This Vulcan plane was surely something to behold. On the Wednesday of that week, King Oliver came to the small regiment. At the guard post, the guard of honour was immaculate. The rest of the camp went down well.

On the platform that was covered on the back and top, King Oliver stood side by side with the Minister President of Germany. They both watched and enjoyed the helicopters and fighting planes as they flew overhead. They also watched soldiers in front of them doing mock-up battles. Communication lines were laid, and instruments set up to show how they worked.

8

Weston And Laura Emigrate to America

WESTON AND LAURA talked quite a lot about emigrating to America. Another four years and the Olympics was due. Over there he could do some good training, and Laura could carry on with her work. After coming back from visiting Evelyn and Cristian, Weston and Laura started to look seriously at what they needed to do in order to get to America. They knew that they had to get an immigration visa or apply for permanent residency. The process would take some time, even up to a year. Then when they get over there, there are immigrants fees to pay plus 'the green card', and also a naturalisation fee.

Weston and Laura were now in full swing getting the papers that they need ready for emigrating. Coming from the football game, they weren't at all pleased the way the club played. They found a cafe and went in for a quick milk shake and a chat, like they always did. Laura said to Weston, "Glad it's all settled now! If it was a communist country, God knows it would have taken years."

"Why would we want to go to a communist country?"

Weston asked looking surprised. "We are going to America, and that's not communist, I'm sure!"

"It just slipped out, don't mean it to be real."

"It's okay, I know what you wanted to say," Weston told her.

"That four hundred metre runner who is from America, in the Olympics, it was very good of him to sponsor us. He has his own training business which comes in very handy for you," Laura told Weston.

"The opportunity presented itself, and I took it. I don't have to worry now about a job. Working and helping out, that's fine, and I could still carry on with my training for the rest of the year's big competitions, and build up for the next Olympics."

"Are you going to try for that one too?" Laura asked. "You should be in top shape by then."

"We should settle in good in California," Weston smiled.

Laura said to Weston, "We read of many people who migrated to America, and have done pretty well, we should do so too."

Weston said, "I think that the first year will be tough for us. Later, we'll be able to get our footing."

"And start a family, you mean," Laura said.

"You want that badly, don't you?" he asked her.

"Of course, when we settle down good and proper. We'll be joining the 40 million there."

It wasn't long before Weston and Laura found themselves at the main airport with their suitcases ready to get on the flight to California. Friends and families came to see them off. The big jumbo jet came in and taxied to the gate Weston and Laura would take, along with all the other passengers.

Los Angeles was a fairly safe place to live. Only in some areas would they find it not safe. Weston and Laura were happy that they had made the decision and picked this place. There were about 27 counties in California. Los Angeles was the capital, and it had a lot to offer. The 400 metres runner from California was named Rod. He showed Weston and Laura around, and also the athletics complex where Weston will be working.

Rod was a decent fellow married and had two children, a boy 10, and a girl of 9. He had worked and trained hard in order to get to the Olympics. Weston was a good runner, and Rod's aim in the next Olympics was to take the title from him. Rod's wife, Margaret, was still at her work when Weston and Laura arrived. Later, she met them and they liked each other straight away. The flat was ready for Weston and Laura and they were driven there to see it. Not too high up in the building, just on the third floor with a beautiful view. It was just what Weston and Laura needed; and were pleased when they saw it.

After a year and a half in California, Weston and Laura decided that it was time to get married. They returned to their home place, and all the wedding plans were made.

King Oliver, Cecilie, Vivianne, and all the other families were there. It was a big posh wedding. Evelyn and Cristian brought the twins, they were now a bit older.

Weston wore a light blue suit with waistcoat and tie. Laura wore a long dress covering her feet, it went up just below the neck, with the arms bare. A long train came from her head and met that of the dress itself. She looked fabulous, like one of those royals. The wedding left many people talking with plenty of pictures to be seen in the top papers. They stayed around a few days then they flew back to California.

Weston didn't tell Laura that when they get back to California, they'll be off on a honeymoon. But it came as a big surprise when she was told about it. She loved the idea, and just couldn't wait to be there. They were going to Laguna Beach just about one hours drive from Los Angeles. A real romantic setting it was. Some of you are probably thinking what happened to Rod, Margaret and the two children. They all were at the wedding. They managed to get a cheap flight there and back. For two weeks Weston and Laura enjoyed their romantic honeymoon, and then came back to face the world.

Having his own athletics set up Rod was moving forward into the big time. Now he also had the 400 metres champion on his team. The stadium had a beautiful track with all the facilities laid out as usual. On the right was a covered stadium. There were many athletes around, and Weston got cracking with some of them. Laura got herself settled in her job, like the people around her, and was content.

9

Prince Bert and Kelly

THE ACTRESS CAME out her front door, closed it and turned the key. She started down the small pathway to the gate, opened it and closed it behind her. It was 8 pm. She was off down to the late night shopping centre which wasn't very far away. The man in the brown suit came up and said to her, "Where is your fancy man then, eh?"

"Go away!" she said. "It's over between you and me. Why are you hanging around here?"

"You know the answer," he told her, "that prince of yours is playing with danger. Coming and taking a man's wife from him. What has he got that I haven't? Is he better in bed than me?"

"He has a lot more than you can show. For a start, he has very good manners, and he behaves himself like a gentleman should."

The man started to laugh, "You can't be serious about the 'gentleman' bit?"

"Why not? Do you know anything about him? Anyway, you're not with me anymore, and that's been done legally. So now, leave me alone! And stop bothering me!"

The man left the actress, turned about and went the other way down the street. The actress met up with Prince Bert at the shopping centre. He had been waiting for her. They went up to the top restaurant and began to talk. "How are you today, Kelly?" he asked, taking her hand into his.

"I'm fine," she told him. "I had a talk with that crazy ex of mine. But he's harmless, full of words."

"Was he bothering you again?" the prince inquired. "Why doesn't he leave you alone? You're a nice woman, too good for him."

"He's not with me anymore, so I don't take it to heart."

After chatting for a while, Prince Bert and Kelly went for a walk.

Kelly told Prince Bert that in two weeks time there'll be the ceremony of the best actors and actresses awards. Kelly said to the prince, "You know that the press will be there in full; and they'll print whatever they can about you."

Prince Bert said, "They've done that before. I'm now accustomed to all that they can dish out."

"That's what you get for being at the top. I'm on the list with three other actresses. This could be my year, let's keep fingers crossed."

Prince Bert said, "You deserve to be actress of the year. You're one of the top actresses around. I'll be there shouting for you."

"So you're definitely coming along?"

"Of course, Ill be with you," the prince told her.

*

Everyone was quiet when the announcer took the list with the names on it for the best actress of the year, and said aloud, "KELLY HAMILTON."

There was lots of applause, cheers and clapping. Kelly left Prince Bert and went up on the stage.

Arriving back from Scotland after a well spent honeymoon, Prince James and Princess Ilka stayed for a few days at the Royal house before going back to the Netherlands. Princess Ilka was fascinated by the beauty of the Highlands. She got a feeling that enraptured her. She said she would definitely take another trip back there. And as for the Loch Ness monster, not a trace of it had she seen. She had longed during her stay to take a photo of this mysterious creature, but it hadn't turned up. Some castles and cathedrals with their architectural makeup was something to see.

"It's a pity you didn't get to see and take a picture of old 'Nessy'. Many people have claimed that they have seen it," King Oliver said to Princess Ilka.

"Maybe on my second trip I'll be able to spot it, and snap it."

"How's your back?" Cecilie asked.

"My rucksack saved me," Princess Ilka told Cecilie. "It was just a slip. But I'm feeling okay now. And James was nice to me, awfully nice. He's a real darling!"

Prince James listening, just smiled and said nothing. Prince James and Princess Ilka knew nothing about Prince Bert leaving. They were given all the news about it, and they found it sad.

King Oliver said, "It should have been that time of year

when the whole house goes up to Scotland for their yearly rest, both you and James could have joined us."

Princess Ilka was listening eagerly. She said, "We missed out this year, hope we'll get to do that some other year. But we don't know what the Dutch have planned. We'll just wait and see."

The last night before Prince James and Princess Ilka flew back to the Netherlands, they were together with King Oliver, Cecilie and Vivianne and others to the opera.

Prince James and Princess Ilka arrived back in the Netherlands just in time for the 'Kings's Day' celebrations. Before, this day was known as 'Queen's Day', but since the prince took over from his mother, it is now known as 'King's Day'. On 'King's Day' everything is orange—the people just like to celebrate their King's Day. And that's exactly what they do.

10

Ascot, and King Oliver Goes to France

ONE OF THE greatest days of the year came around. It was the day of Ascot known as *'Ladies Day'* by a poet. Queen Anne was out riding one day when she saw a spot that would be fine for the horses to stretch their legs. This was in 1711. James II was the father of Queen Anne; she was the second daughter. She was pregnant 17 times and managed to bring forth a boy whose name was William. He died of smallpox only 11 years old. Queen Anne was 37 when she took the throne. During her reign, the United Kingdom of Great Britain came about with England joining with Scotland. A race hosted under Queen Anne's reign was called *Her Majesty's Plate*.

On this day of Ascot, men and women could dress up, and go out and show themselves. Of course, one had to dress decently, not having the dress too short and showing too much of the breasts. The women wore fancy hats, some out of this world. Most men would wear suits and bowlers, carrying umbrellas. Children were allowed if accompanied by an adult.

This day at Ascot is also about the Royal house and its members being there. The first carriage arrives with

King Oliver, Cecilie and Vivianne. All the other carriages followed behind, waving to the crowds as they went along. Cecilie broke the news to the king that she was pregnant. They celebrated there. The racecourse at Ascot is about 9.7 km long. The king and his attendants failed to win anything.

King Oliver with his attendants boarded the ferry at Dover which would take him to Calais. The journey wasn't long, just over 1 hour and 20 minutes. Cecilie and Vivianne also went along. The king met the President of France and later opened a music institute. The king and his attendants spent a week in France.

On the way back, the day started off fine, bright and sunny, then there were dark clouds covering the skies. Great winds started up, and there was a great storm. Enormous waves came from the blowing of extreme winds, and the ferry was caught, capsized and sunk. It happened so suddenly, the helicopters that were nearby, couldn't do a thing. Everyone on that ferry drowned. It was a terrible tragedy. The news went around the world like a flash. The main papers in the country were filled with the story:

> **'KING AND ALL HIS ATTENDANTS, WIFE AND ADOPTED MOTHER DROWNED IN FERRY.'**

Prince James was next in line to take the throne but he had given up his British Nationality in order to marry Princess Ilka of the Netherlands. Now it was not possible for him to be king.

The old king had a brother, Prince Robert who was much younger, and was next in line to take the throne. I think that the people of the country were glad too, because they had no real liking for Prince James as king. Prince Robert, lived with his wife Cheryll and their young son Wilfred. They always attended everything that had to do with the Royal house.

Sheila's mother was watching TV while Sheila herself was in the kitchen. There came on a news flash. Sheila's mum stood there staring at it, and not believing the news. She cried out and Sheila heard the cry and went to investigate. Her mum was holding both her hands to her face, and shaking her head. "It's my grandson," she said. "It's my grandson. *HE'S DEAD!*"

"What are you talking about?" Sheila said. "The king has gone over to France for a short visit...and..." Hearing the news of the tragedy, tears came from her eyes as she consoled her mother.

Weston had just come back from the athletics training. He entered the living room, switched the TV on, and was shocked when he heard what they were talking about. It was his brother, the King. He was drowned in the ferry coming back from France. Weston sat down with a saddened face and continue to listen to the news.

Playing with the twins, Evelyn turned around to face Cristian who had been out in the barn, and had heard the shocking news on the small radio. She saw on his face that he was upset. "Is everything okay?" she asked.

He took her by the hand and sat her down. "It is your brother," he told her. "He went down with the ferry coming back from France." He told her the whole story, and she began to weep.

Funeral arrangements were made as according to the customs of the country. All the governments and other nations were told about it. The body of the King was guarded by four soldiers. Flags in the country flew half mast. Bells tolled. Prince Robert, who has now become king, will speak to the country. There'll be a parade from the Royal house down the Mall and past the Cenotaph. The coffin will go to Westminster Hall, and will lie in state for four days. The public are allowed to come and pay their respects.

After about nine days, the funeral will take place. The body is moved from Westminster Hall to Westminster Abbey. There's a tradition going back to Queen Victoria where the coffin is pulled on a green gun carriage by 138 sailors.

The country was back in a happy mood with the coronation of King Robert. His wife Cheryl became Queen Consort. Much prosperity came to the country while Robert was king. His reign was a good one, and the people were pleased with him.

The End

Also by John Gumbs

Jehanne 978-1-78222-571-3
The Trial and Burning of Jehanne 978-1-78222-609-3
Aitch H 978-1-78222-628-4
Jay G 978-1-78222-656-7
Heidi 978-1-78222-682-6